THE LIGHTKEEPER'S LOVER

MOLLIE MATHEWS

Blue Orchid
PUBLISHING

Based on true events

OVERVIEW

**When their world crashes,
will their love meet the test?**

A woman who flees from love and a man who can't keep it.

These two lonely people couldn't picture a life where love ever stayed. A legacy of painful secrets and wounds unspoken.

Set in New Zealand, *The Lightkeeper's Lover* is a beautifully moving story of love, loss and betrayal, and what we have to do to heal our hearts.

A delightful mystical romance with a dream-like quality that weaves fantasy and myth into everyday life.

AUTHOR'S NOTE

Thanks so much for reading my contemporary romance, *The Lightkeeper's Lover.*

It's a lot different in style and tone than my other books, but I do like to experiment. The story was inspired by my own experiences and the love affair I once had with a former US Navy Seal.

I've always believed in the power of creativity and art to heal and I've included this as a theme in this story. You might say *The Lightkeeper's Lover* has more of a magical realism tone, and some readers have described it as 'poetic' but, I'll let you decide.

The Lightkeeper's Lover is a short story, and like all my short stories and full-length romances it contains the theme of heartbreak, family, destiny and the power of love to heal.

I hope you love the story. Some people loved the beginning best, some loved the end, and other's the whole thing. There's something for everyone in this story.

Read to the end for a free excerpt from my full-length book, *Married By Christmas,* and learn more about Issy, the art therapist, who you'll meet in the last chapter of this book.

As a special bonus, I've also included advance chapters from my full-length book, *Claimed by the Sheikh,* due for release in 2019. You'll meet some of the hero's friends and learn more about his royal lineage.

PRAISE FOR THE LIGHTKEEPER'S LOVER

"This is not my normal genre but you made the lighthouse come alive. *The Lightkeeper's Lover* was an enjoyable and quick read that drew me in from the first page to the last. The lighthouse took on human characteristics or personification and was almost poetic in his thoughts. When Lucy was on the cliff near the lighthouse, she was in so much despair and was hurt and angry when not offered shelter. The epilogue was a surprise and was unexpected but welcomed since it fleshed out the story. "

~ JoAnne W.

"*The Lightkeeper's Lover* has a lovely mystical, poetic feel about it, with deep longings being experienced by the characters."

~ **Advance review.**

"Evocative, emotional and lyrical are some of the words that come to mind as I read this short story. There are moments in life when one cannot explain the deep feelings the rise up and overcome one, bringing about an almost mystical connection. As the lighthouse and the girl call out to each other in their pain, an emotional attraction paves the path to her future. The final chapter in the book brings the story together in a charming way and one is relieved at the outcome. "

~ Margaret Watkins

*For Lorenzo, who brings love to life,
and to all the men and women who have devoted their lives to the
protection of others.*

LEARNING LOVE AND LOVE AND LOVE

"We're the bridge across forever, arching above the sea, adventuring for our pleasure, living mysteries for the fun of it, choosing disasters triumphs challenges impossible odds, testing ourselves over and again, learning love and love and love!"

~ Richard Bach~

The woman wandering the cliff tops grew weary from her broken heart and sat, weeping, at the base of the lighthouse.

She wore the cloak of a betrayed lover, looking lost and forlorn, wondering whether one day love would come to stay.

Through teary eyes she looked to the heavens, beseeching, "Why hath thou forsaken me?"

The lighthouse, unaware of her presence, stood tall and solid, gazing sadly out to sea. Grieving he searched vainly for his lover. Waiting. Waiting for the lover never meant to be.

Two souls lonely in their loss, united by the yearning for love that would stay, remained unaware of each other and saw not that which lay within the distance of touch.

The heavens sought to intervene—orchestrating the elements to throw them further together.

Violet-gray clouds swirled angrily—gaining momentum. Faster and faster. The woman stumbled to her feet as the wind rose.

Finally noticing the presence of the lighthouse, she ran to its door and tried to open it. The handle, stiff from lack of use, refused to succumb to her touch.

She persisted—pounding on the cold, steel door, determined in her knowledge and belief that, despite the cold exterior, inside it would be warm.

The lighthouse stood firm, unyielding. And yet his curiosity was aroused. Secretly he bent to see her, looking with soft, kindly eyes—wanting to let her in, yet fearful of the returning feelings. Fearful of the stirring in his heart.

Fearful of her.

What if she came in, settled, filled the house with her scent, her song—filling the void which for so long he had denied existed.

He had got used to his own company. He had to to survive. To be alone somehow seemed more bearable than to admit to love lost and to try again. Years earlier his love had left for the sea, wrenching at his heart and causing him more torment than he had ever thought possible, and yet he had not shed a tear.

"Lighthouses are strong, they do not cry," he had said to

himself as he farewelled his deserting lover cordially. As she had sailed into the distance the tears had welled in his eyes but he hardened his heart and scolded himself for his weakness.

Yet whenever the rain came he released those tears he kept pent up inside. In the rain his tears would go unnoticed, indistinguishable from the drops that fell from the sky.

But tonight, as he heard the woman's cries, heard her pleas and the pounding fists to come inside, he felt those tugs upon his heart again. Despite his desire to discard his suit of armor he steeled himself as though preparing for an attack. His heart hardened, and the door remained shut.

The pounding grew weaker until finally, he watched her walk away.

His heart sunk. Despite all his armor she had managed to penetrate his fortress and something about her had awakened feelings he thought had died.

He wanted to call to her, "Do not give up on me so easily —knock upon my door just one more time," yet his lips remained firmly pursed.

He watched as she walked to the edge of the cliff, weeping, cold, frightened—so in need of warmth, hugs, and affection. His arms wanted to go to her, yet they remained formless, stoic, at his side. His feet wanted to run to her — anticipating the fate that fell before her. Yet they remained firmly encased in stone.

His light wanted to shine on her, to warn her, to beckon her, "Come back, come back, stay with me. I will keep you, protect you, care for you."

Yet his will was subverted by the force of habit. The beam of light disappeared according to its programmed instructions. The wind danced around him, twisting and turning, darting and diving—seeking to awaken him, urging him, "Live as though you have little time my friend—do not let history repeat."

He saw her only momentarily, as the light returned, standing at the edge of the cliff arms outstretched.

Desperately be willed himself to deny his programming and allow the light to stay—hoping to trap her in its rays as a hunter traps its prey. Hoping to save her from the fate that lay before her. He struggled as the great bulbs of light ached and groaned, straining to shut down.

"NOOOOOOOO!" he screamed as she was engulfed in darkness.

2

———

Darkness. His long-trusted friend, maternal confidant and disguised enemy all wrapped into a singular umbilical cord. Familiar tomes of survival, aging, duty, and numbness served to help the cogs of the great mechanism direct the powerful beam back out to sea, where it should have been before...

She.

The light once again splayed out—arcing toward the

faithful waters of the ocean. As the beam circled, its clarity noticeably blurred. Noticeably weakened. Noticeably fainted.

Why here? Why now? Why did she come to this lighthouse, this solitary station?

She could have taken shelter in any number of warm doorways and tavern hearths. Was she lost? Why had the pain of her loss, her need for warmth, light, and love, driven her far out to this godforsaken desolate place?

Why take such a risk, such a journey—passing by the welcoming arms of those that might seek to harbor her? Harbor her momentarily, maybe. Perhaps long enough to dry out her melancholic drenched heart—if only to then commence her search.

But why this damned rock?

The reluctant glimpse he had taken of her was but a quick glance. Yet what he stole in an instant became sealed in bronze, seared as an image, scorched into his mind. Those swollen, seeping eyes, those heaving breasts, so filled with feelings to feel and the desperate desire to be needed.

How does such a beautiful woman, so apparently spiritual, so apparently grounded, take flight? What has the world done to one so sensitive? One so precious? Who answers to that condemnation, who answers to the charges I lay before this question, he wondered?

An uncaring and selfish man? A bitter and jealous family? Maybe I have lived too long alone to know the injustices that befall lovely and lonely women the world over.

Have I been gone that long? Have I been so out of touch as to not feel her approaching my bastion of perceived strength? I should have felt her timid footsteps on my anchor of granite. I should have sensed her meekness. I should have...

Felt her.

What?

NO!

Don't ask it.

NO!

What has happened to me over these years?

As the realization began to dawn over the giant dome that housed the aging mirrors, the great light dimmed as the moment of atonement anchored.

Many years before he had chosen his path. Countless years previous, he had chosen this life.

His modus was gallantry, honor, a sense of achievement. He would save lives, and experience the best that a mortal man could serve in a lifetime.

Love, life, war, pain, and peace in equal measure. As much as was readily available. And with those newly acquired experienced eyes, he would then know how best to act as a sentinel in the night. To protect those that came close to danger. He had chosen to put himself in danger's way. Deliberately. To learn what one should do.

This, he thought would be all that he needed to help others and those he loved to assuage their pain, their senseless actions and struggles with the weight of the world.

Idealism....youthful idealism. Pride, stubbornness, naivety —call it what you will. Septic lacerating reality is the plague of the dreamer, the idealist. With that reality comes the death of innocence, and the return of balance and clarity.

Idealism turns to pessimism. The world, once a wondrous, unique and welcoming entity, turned into a greedy, capitalistic, inhumane and sadistic sentence which one must serve with impunity.

What the hell happened to me?

Why can I not tap into those never-ending cleansing energies that served me so well in my youth?

What the hell happened to me?

It was that very question that had lingered under the surface for years. In the daytime, when the lighthouse shut down and was off duty, it festered subcutaneously waiting for the call to protect and rescue, as he himself was in need of rescue.

And it was her pounding in the night that allowed the primordial bridge to be created and the question to traverse from day to night—to now.

To shift in awareness from subconscious secrecy to supreme mind-share.

Those damned small, insistent clenched fists. What nature of pain did they hold for them to be so different? Different from others who had tried in vain to breech his fortress. Different from the pain of his stoically guarded memories. Yes, memories aplenty.

So, let's pick one of many.

Say...

No, not that.

Say...

No, not those.

My wife. Maybe.

Yes. I can go there.

My beautiful loving wife. That soft and tender smile, her sensual touch, her innocent youth—so full of love, promises, dreams, and hope. Socialized from birth to play the ideal role. What killed our love? Why did I not now wake up beside her inviting lips, her wonderfully tepid skin and the musky smell of our lovemaking the sunset previous? What killed that?

Let's see...

The war maybe?

My training was supposed to make me impenetrable, wise and wary. What happened that horrific month in that humid bloody valley? The tree-lines simmering in the Panamanian heat... snipers picking off those that could not find cover.

The fear, the baptism of deliverance, and then that beast that overtook me—serving only to warrant the post-op psychiatric evaluation. And the unspoken notoriety of the wounded and dead that numbed my conscience from that day forward.

Maybe that killed my love.

Or maybe they're all just symptoms. Symptoms of a boy who went seeking the world and found it. The eclipsed side. Shown to him in a dark soliloquy through the tempestuous wrath of an impatient and imprudent god.

Damn him, and damn reminiscing.

Memories, be gone! Be gone!

3

———

I need to concentrate on getting my beam back to full strength. Main drive engaged. Cogs check. Main relays and busses confirmed operational...right. Now let's check the interior. Mirrors aligned, fuses intact, element primed. Right. Beam powering up, strength and luminosity regaining maximum consistency...right. Full strength reached. Check completed. Back to normal operation.

Whew...back to normal.

Whew...back to normal.

Whew...back to normal.

The great saber of light once again arced out across the bay, swinging back and forth. The relapse of conscience fading fast. Then there was silence.

Silence changed utterance, utterance to subtlety, subtlety to subtle urgency, and that to the slow crescendo of metal straining against metal. The grinding of cogs, forcing them to rebel against their programmed counterparts.

The great beam swung toward the rocks. Towards the last known position of the beautiful, brief angel. The powerful dome came to a grinding halt at the summit of the rock face.

The questions and yearning to know overpowering the mechanical automation of normalcy.

For a second the beam stayed affixed on the summit. Nothing came into focus. The summit was cold and devoid of her. She was not there.

Despair.

The beam reluctantly tracked down the cliff-face towards the perilous rocks at the bottom. The face of the cliff turned a pungent brown with the attention of the great Illuminati. The beam finally reached the bottom. She was nowhere to be discovered.

Despair.

A feeling came to the lighthouse. A feeling of being tricked, seconded, seduced by emotion, and hope and wonderment meant for maybe poets or a youth now squandered in the irretractable past.

Nevertheless, a powerful shudder was felt deep within the foundation of the great structure and for once...openly... honestly....he wept.

Mechanical and spiritual tears entwined, sliding slowly

down the formidable shaft...for he reluctantly longed to regain what he had lost through this fragile portal of life and love and hope that had come pounding at his door, promising to heal his cold, salt-encrusted impenetrable soul.

Was the beautiful savior only a visage?

4

She heard his questions and they were worthy ones indeed—ones she asked of herself, for she had been there before: the great divide between good and evil, helping and hurting. Never intending the hurting, but it had come. Always come. Just as with a storm comes rain. With love...with love always comes pain. And yet it didn't have to be this way.

Lightness and darkness. Good and evil. Deception and truth.

So many questions raised. So many assumptions made. Was she a savior or was she a temptress supreme – breaking down barriers he had erected for sound reason; pacing the parameters of his being; picking at the mortar until this formidable structure crumbled.

She remembered words said to her once by a seer: "Yours is the lesson of love. It is not that you have never been loved. Some people spend all their lives never, ever having been loved. This is not the case with you."

This had both frightened her and intrigued her. Was the lesson hers to learn, or to teach? To teach others how to be loved or to learn this for herself? She had decided it was hers to teach. It suited her better. It felt safer.

However, slowly and painfully she had realized that the things we have to learn are very rarely the things we choose. For despite setting forth to teach and having taught those she loved how to be loved, having loved them with all her heart, having wrapped their whole being with the blanket of her soul, at the point where she was closest to succeeding she grew restless, discontented, afraid.

Just at the point when they were ready to love her as she had loved them, she changed, backed off. Instead of being their support she became critical, distant, unaccepting— provoking them to abandon her. Therein affirming her belief, her reality, that love never stays.

She couldn't picture a life where it did.

But that was before...

Before the day a man came into her life who radiated such a zest for living, who laughed and danced and *knew* how to love, filling her world with deep, blissful tenderness.

They would lie in bed together oblivious to the rest of

the world, making love to the sensuous melody of Oscar Peterson. Entwining their being together, immersed in the musical symphony.

"Now I've got you I'm never going to lose you," her lover said, cementing his promise with a ring.

A promise of love to stay.

Until it didn't.

5

For a while she was happy, feeling safe, protected with this man she so deeply loved, who told her she was beautiful every night and every day.

For a while she was happy with this man who laughed and danced, whose voice rang with merriment, joy and happiness. This man whose piano playing would float through the house and bless the weary ears of those who lived down the valley.

So happy was she that she hadn't noticed that the merriment always stemmed from the glass never far from his hand.

So happy was she that she hadn't noticed the mask so subtle in appearance that it merged effortlessly from the darkness of night into the brightness of day.

So happy was she that she did not realize the effort that went into sustaining the appearance of everlasting joy.

She hadn't noticed until the cracks started appearing, expanding rapidly into crevices before she had a chance to protect herself from harm.

Crevices which plummeted rapidly to the raging torrents below. Torrents not of water but filled with snakes and worms and maggots and leeches which sucked mercilessly at one so full of life and love.

She had thrown a life-line to him but he rejected it defiantly, his tortured eyes looking at her as though possessed. Hating her, provoking her to hate him. She felt like a parent thrown into the seas with her child, struggling to rescue him, seeing his weakness, knowing that he had resigned himself to impending death, wanting to reach him, to shake him, loving him too much to walk away.

The words reluctantly omitted from his lips forever etched in her mind.

"I'm afraid," he cried.

Years later she came to see the lesson in this for her. For in him she saw herself mirrored—a resemblance that only emerged as she reassembled the shattered pieces of her life.

Who was she to presume to teach others to love or to be loved when she had never mastered it herself? Who was she to assume a position of superiority when really she had no idea—running every time when those she purported to love loved her back? Sabotaging again, and again, and again, her hopes of happiness.

These things she pondered as she lay on the clifftop that night, looking at the stars. She felt glad and sad in equal measure that she had come to her senses and was not now lying 100 meters on the jagged rocks below.

"Damn that lighthouse", she shouted to the wind, luring her out to this wild, desolate spot, then abandoning her, pretending not to be in, denying that he had led her here.

For just when she had given up, resigning herself to the grayness of the landscape, the mediocrity of life, the broken-ness of those she loved, a beacon of light had emerged.

Entrancing her, capturing her interest not with a rainbow promising gold but a glimmer of hope to the future.

A voice had immediately warned her to keep her distance. To run. To stay away. She knew this voice well enough to heed it and so away she stayed.

But the light would reappear from time to time. There was something about its glow that made it difficult to see if the route was safe and so she lay there and waited.

6

As she walked along the cliffs, the beacon of light had been so radiant, so pure, so cleansed that as a moth goes to the lamp so she was drawn. She bypassed the welcoming arms of those who sought to shelter her, ignoring the promises from others to love, cherish and hold.

"Be careful" the winds had called but she walked on in defiance.

"This time it will be different. I've learnt my lesson, I won't make the same mistakes," she had reassured the Fates.

She resented her confidence now. She resented him.

"Damn him! Damn him! I've been fooled again—destined to repeat the test until I learn the lesson," she admonished.

Why did he have to shine his light so brightly, transmitting unspoken messages of safety, warmth and protection? Yet in the same breath refusing to let her come inside?

Only so close, so close, was she allowed.

No more. No less.

Why did it have to be so hard? She just wanted to walk inside. Suddenly realization dawned. She saw it now—the pattern of her lovers: the closed doors, the encased hearts. The challenge they presented. The work they required.

She saw how she had been offered glimpses of what could be. Intermittent reinforcement but never the devotion and courage required to deliver everlasting love.

Devoid of the courage to be vulnerable and to commit to mutual healing, the men she loved could never weather the fiercest of storms.

She saw now that she attracted into her life people who had the most to teach her and who reflected those parts of herself that she denied. Like attracts like. Her door, she knew, was not as easily opened as she believed.

She was afraid to open her heart.

As she lay on the ground staring at the stars she challenged the heavens, "Give me a sign. Give me a sign that I am on track. Give me a sign that I'm progressing, learning, growing. Please tell me what to do. Please tell me I'm not destined to spin in my tracks, continually making the wrong choices in life, continually loving the wrong men."

At that moment the beam of light glided across her, just

missing the rise of her breasts. Her heart quickened as she saw the pinnacle of light veer off course, looking not out to sea, but tentatively tracking down the cliff-face.

He was searching.

Searching for her.

She turned her head gently not wanting to alert him to her presence. She wanted to watch him, and to stay within this miraculous and most unexpected moment. She wanted to be sure that it was true.

It was then that she saw the tears and his shuddering form. Sensing his despair, she felt a great wave of love connect them. She wanted to call out to him, "I'm here! I'm here!" But she lay there paralyzed. Caught once again in the divide of lightness and darkness, good and evil, deception and truth.

And then the light disappeared.

7

The woman who lay strewn on the cliff-top grew weary from her waiting. Waiting to be discovered by one who chose not to discover her. Waiting for the love that never came.

She closed her heart to the man who chose not to harbor her. Who chose to ignore the strength of the bond that was never ignited. Who chose darkness over light.

There's no point grieving for that which was not

destined to be she decided, as she picked herself up, regained her composure and fortified herself to embrace her next encounter.

Something deep within her had changed that night.

Her heart quickened as before her eyes a path she had not seen before appeared. She skipped off full of excitement and optimism. In the distance she could hear a laughing child and the voice of a man, wiser, older, less tainted by the past.

And she knew, she just knew, that once again life had been kind to her. For the lessons we have to learn are rarely those we would choose.

8

Half way down the path she paused, not wanting to but somehow unable to stop the backward glance. She saw the lighthouse standing in the shadows, solid in his stance, isolated in his loneliness.

Yet she felt not pity, but anger. Her optimism drained from her body as hope drains from one who feels betrayed. It zapped her life force and slowed her breathing, making it difficult to turn the other cheek and walk away.

A tear forced itself from her eye, and she quickly caught it before it began its long, slow descent down her cheek, taunting her with its determination to summon others.

She did not want to give him the satisfaction of seeing her cry, to let him know that he still held such power over her, to let him know he had such control. She was determined her anger should not be contained.

Or, she wondered, was anger her way of channeling her pain, her disappointment and her sorrow?

Perhaps in the lighthouse she saw herself—lonely, isolated and impenetrable. Attracting others toward her bright light and then repelling them when they got too close, as the rocks repel the ships who seek the safety of its shore.

Bruising them as they, and all those that lie within its bows are thrown again, and again against the rocks. Rescuing no one, only warning them and punishing those who seek to defy the warning. Like an angry sea which silently grows stronger, more menacing in its depth and wake.

How quickly her optimism and sunny disposition had left her, she thought. How quickly the seas can turn.

Directing her anger inward now, she chastised herself for having been tricked again. Tricked by the promises of mere mortals who knew with predictable accuracy the words which most beguile.

I love you.

Words, only words, yet spoken so convincingly, assuaging her melancholic, disbelieving heart.

This she struggled with. Blatant trickery —telling her only what they knew she wanted to hear, then incredulous and defiant that these words should come back to haunt them when she asked them to keep their promise.

She found it difficult to speak her truth—the depth of her feelings so powerful and so rich. For as long as she could remember her passion was buried deep. Trusting no one with the key. Trusting no one with the truth.

Several times she had offered a map, lay down before those who promised to care, but always she would be disappointed by their reluctance to stay the distance.

Other jewels seem to glimmer brighter, perhaps requiring less effort than she with her complicated heart. In the end all she could do was accept that perhaps she was not the priceless gem that others had led her to believe.

Her anger she now directed to those, and particularly to him, who had once again carried her high within the currents of hope, promise, and wonderment, only to abandon her as they reached the summit.

But had she been abandoned?

Or was it a case of abandoning? She could not be sure. The sadness and heaviness in her heart was the only feeling that carried some certainty. To survive she knew that she had to go on, trying to fathom the complexity that lay within and that would, until healed, lead her toward a similar fate. Again and again.

It was hard work and required both a fervent imagination and a deep trust in the course of life she knew could not be manipulated.

Could it be, she wondered, that all is well? That everything was working toward her highest good?

Only time would tell.

9

———

"Finally!" he thought. There she was. A spectacle to behold in his bright light.

A beauty.

His Queen.

Yet why was she walking away? The lighthouse did not understand. Was this trickery? A game? The rules of which he did not know and a part he did not know if it was his to play.

Her angry face and clenched fists confused and worried him. The pupils of her eyes, once huge in wonderment, now dilated in anger and despair.

Her hurt stirred up feelings he sought to quell stirred feelings and memories long since buried. How dare she? How dare she toy with him?

She had caused him to abandon his station, his post. She had caused him to forsake the trust that others had placed in him to protect. To be stable, solid, predictable—unwavering in the protection he offered to those who sort his shelter.

His great beam of light flickered, straining under the weight of times past.

"Women, what is it with women?" he beseeched the heavens, his fists clenched, yet stoic by his side, at the recollection of similar trickery.

His heart felt as if would explode under the frustration of it all. He who understood the currents of the sea, the cycles of the moon, the regularity within which ships would call, could not understand this creature who had stood defiantly before him.

His heart wrestled to analyze the situation, the behavior, to attribute motive, reason, and logic to that which threatened to beguile, robbing him of his peace, decimating his love of solitude.

For now, now, against his wishes, his heart, not his head, sought to over-ride the controls. He could not, would not, should not, let her go.

His head spun with heated debate, running through all the possible causes for her hurtful behavior. His heart conducted the orchestra of emotion into heightened crescendo.

The symbols within his soul, long since dormant,

banged and clanged with gusto, reverberating against his heart as a runaway hub cap spins upon an icy road. Trumpets of thunder rose to a climax. The noise was deafening to his ear, obliterating the words of logic and reason that sort to soothe him and offer him the solace of his mind.

There would be no solace. Not again. He was caught. Caught in the canyon where the river of love roared, separated by the cliffs of love and hate.

His frustration and the torturous symphony stopped abruptly as the woman wandering the clifftops turned her face up toward his light. He saw the sadness which lay etched in her face and the pool of water threatened to overflow from her great blue eyes.

He realized at once... at once... her pain.

He wanted to take her in his arms, to offer her words of comfort, to clarify the misunderstanding that lay deep inside. He would have, could have, had she lingered just that bit longer.

"Why would I hurt you?" He called to her, but his words fell short of her ears. Her fleeing form gave no clue as to whether or not he had been heard.

10

"Now he shows," she cried.

Now, when I have all but given up on him. Forgotten him. Damn him, damn him and his words which sought an answer.

Yes, she had heard him, but what was the point in stopping to answer? That would be folly—laying her open to more tricks, more lies and deceit.

She hesitated. But, what if, what if he truly did not seek

harm, she wondered? What if his question was an innocent one? What if he did not understand? What if he did not mirror the ways of the others who had broken her heart?

Impossible. Impossible. Impossible. They are made of the same iron. At least the ones she had sought refuge from. Their scripts, their stories, their endings were similar in so many ways.

But this tall bastion of courage and fortitude—why had he impacted her so? Was he, too, not sheltering from his past, seeking to heal in the waters of isolation? Seeking to strengthen himself away from the path where others may tread, interfering with his healing by ripping at the carcass of his wounds?

Wounds still raw from the recent ravages of war and love. Picking at the delicious bulk of his form, circling him with their lust and longing. Forsaking him once they had fed greedily on his soul. Wanting to take their memories of time spent with one so unique and majestic but leaving nothing in return.

Did he seek only to contain not to liberate? But can another liberate or give life to one whose breath is shallow and whose pulse has gone weak? Can one in hibernation be revitalized by one who experiences the sun? Or is energy transferred like an imbalanced equation—one growing stronger at the expense of the other? One awakening as the other slowly dies?

She didn't know. She only knew that they were both in despair now. Not much had changed since they first met, only that unlike before, now they were aware of each others presence, their wounds and their fears.

Yet, rather than heal each other, still he refused to open his heart, and she had grown weary from her wait.

11

He looked at her disdainfully, scornfully and with mocking in his heart. So often as the summit is in sight those that seek its glory give up.

Silly, foolish woman. How easy it is to play with your heart. How easy and predictably you fall. One sweet word here, one silent pause there and you can be manipulated like the limbs of a fly in the hands of a child—your soul twisted unmercifully without respite.

Why do I bother ? You have been rescued and yet you do not perceive it? I never promised to stay.

Again, and again I have shone my light of warning. Again, and again I have set you on your path, picked you up, redirected you. Yet again, and again you look back and return to this path as though you felt there were no other.

Do you have the brain of a human or the intellect of a lab rat? Why do you persist in seeing more in others than exists? Why do you continue believing more than can be witnessed, touched and evidenced?

Optimism. I tire of it.

The realm of make believe is for poets, artists and those whose hearts lie heavy and burdened by their imaginary lives.

Wake up! Wake up and run away quickly. Stop burdening me with your tears, clenched fists and limpet-like nature. I carry no one and no one carries me. What need have I of your company?

Others will come. Others less battered by the seas and the torrents of their past. My light is for the clean, sleek ships that pass in the night. And if I choose, I may lure them, trick them and beguile them into false security.

That is fun, a nice deviation from the boredom that duty dictates. I am sick of my post but, as yet, I have no where to go. You have been a nice break in my routine but little challenge and if I am to be honest, very little to behold. Why would I want a spent vessel like you?

Go away. You repulse me!

No wait! Don't go. Not yet. I'm sorry. I didn't mean to offend. My words were uttered carelessly. They fell from my lips yet I know not where they were formed.

My hurt? My wounds? My pain? I know them all. I offer them as no excuse.

You are my family. The person I am closest to. My only love...please understand. I know you are cross now but in time, if I allow you time, you will cool down, you will forgive me...you care about me too much to remain angry. We enjoy each other too much. It is only when we are apart that we are cruel...

That I am cruel...

Please say you understand.

12

The woman once defiant in her anger knew not how to respond. The lighthouse's behavior confused her and brought out the worst parts of her personality.

His words, both soothing and scorching, bounced around the sides of her head like belted jeans tumbling in a dryer. The clanging becoming louder with every word uttered. The heated emotions becoming increasingly dangerous and insidious like a gas building up, unseen by the naked, rational eye.

Yet again, like a moth to a flame she was drawn and no matter how she resisted she could not. She imagined herself in a row boat without oars, her friends with arms outstretched trying to reach her. And he, with his big, steady beam, enticing her, illuminating her way, beguiling her with his brightness.

Or was it just that by shining his light she was able to see what others could not? Was it the brightness of the light that lead to the wisdom within? Or was this a thought born in folly itself?

And why was she in that row boat at all?

This was a good question and one she should have pondered earlier.

13

It was over. She had resisted him for so long until finally giving in, giving in to his advances against her will. Her will was weak, vulnerable to his soft, soothing words, and promises of affection.

And so she had reluctantly agreed to go to him. As the time when they would again be together drew closer she felt herself become excited and her imagination ran through how wonderful the night would be.

Her body trembled with anticipation and her lips grew moist with desire. Skepticism and caution fled her body and emptied from her mind as she drank thirstily from the bowl of her imagination and the memories of time spent together.

That the call should come should not have surprised her. She should have been better prepared. Yet she was starved of affection and before her lay a banquet of desire. She did not think to slow her consumption.

Disbelieving she still did not accept his warning that he may not come. Could not come.Would not come.

There was still hope.

Wasn't there?

14

———

HOPE. High Outlook Proving Empty. The bowl of her imagination harbored nothing but the ashes of times past that would never be revisited and were impure in their form.

But the winds of faith carried with them a special seed, from which sprung magic. The imagery and wonderment was not unlike the phoenix rising from the ashes, or of the lotus blossoming from the murky swamp beyond.

Every day the pain was far less and soon it would fade altogether. Just as the delirious cry from a woman post child birth who is adamant she will never experience the pain again, with certainty would come more suffering but its stay would be shorter and somewhat sweeter in its brevity.

She had healed her heart. She had seen the light. She had heard the warning.

The lighthouse couldn't love.

Not yet. Perhaps not ever. His wounds were so deep, his love of isolation and solitary nature so entrenched.

But he had shown her that hope could have another meaning.

Her optimism returned and proved eternal.

She would love again.

Wouldn't she?

EPILOGUE

"Did you paint that? It's incredible. I'm in awe." The man's deep velvet voice held just a trace of a Middle-Eastern accent and the tone made Lucy blush. Not because of the compliment, but the way the man's voice resonated with every artery in her heart. If there was a sexier voice in the world she'd never heard it.

Barely conscious of the crowd pressing around her

Lucy's heart quickened as she scanned the tall, dark, thoroughly captivating stranger, trailing her eyes the length of his 6 foot two inch frame. Broad-shouldered and formidable, the starkly moulded framework of his face spotlighted by the curated gallery lights. He exuded authority and a compelling magnetism that sent her pulse soaring.

Clutching the exhibition catalogue to her chest Lucy turned from him and swept her gaze over the crowd crammed into the art gallery. Pulse pounding, she tried to catch the attention of Issy Riley, the art therapist, who had encouraged her to paint her way to healing. But Issy was deep in conversation with her husband, Massimilliano Balforni, CEO of Emporio Balforni, Milan's most prestigious fashion house, the man Issy had met and married after helping him heal his wounds too.

Lucy loved the easy way they were together and the deep love they obviously shared. She wished she could have a love like that. A love that weathered even the roughest storm. A love that shone with such a bright light.

Heat shot through her as her awareness returned to the absurdly handsome stranger beside her. Lucy shifted her gaze from Issy and Max and fixed her sight on the stark white wall closest to the door. On the white panel was her name in gold letters, Lucy Ford, and the title of the show, *The Lightkeeper's Lover*.

"Of course you painted it," the stranger said, following her gaze momentarily, before turning to her, his dark umber eyes magnetically pulling hers to his. "This is a solo exhibition and you are the star."

They both smiled, as though sharing in the surprise of their chance encounter and immediate attraction, causing her heart to somersault.

"The weather blew me in," he said, as though offering an explanation.

She looked over the sea of heads to the sky, watching in fascination as the violet-gray clouds swirled angrily outside. Gaining momentum. Faster. And faster.

Just as they had—

Lucy's breath caught in her chest as her thoughts travelled back to that haunting night so many years ago. Back to that desolate evening when she had wandered the clifftops, straddled between wanting to live and wanting to die. Back to that night when she had been rescued from the fate that was never meant to be hers.

Why had this bastion of strength come striding into her life? It was if the heavens had sought to intervene again—orchestrating the elements to throw them together.

"The title of your show drew me, and I was curious. Then I saw your paintings—wow! What can I say. It's exactly how it is. You've captured the emotion exactly."

"You're being kind," Lucy said, unused to such direct praise. Unexpectedly, her eyes pooled with tears. She didn't know why. She just hoped she wouldn't cry.

"No, really. The desolation. The loneliness. The isolation. But also the connection. You've taken it further, you've seen below the surface—the hope, the healing, and the beauty."

His gaze from her to the painting at the entrance, running along the soaring cliffs troughed on the canvas with a hurtle of white and ochre and veins of gold. His gaze honed in on the hauntingly beautiful face of a woman, infused within the rocks. Then rose along the formidable shaft of the lighthouse, its beam of light towering over her like a protector.

"You have a rare ability to capture emotion," he said,

turning to her again. "I knew you had to be mine." Dark eyes, deep and solid as crystal held her spellbound.

He laughed, the sort of easy laugh that only those with supreme confidence in themselves managed when revealing their unconscious thoughts. "What I meant was, I knew I had to buy one of your paintings and make it mine."

He gestured toward the largest painting on display by the door, shining like a beacon, attracting people struggling along the streets away from the wild Wellington winds and raging rain battering them mercilessly.

At just over two meters high, the painting was exactly the same commanding height as her admirer.

Lucy felt a tug of conflict, a type of regret but also pleasure as the gallery owner placed a red sticker below the painting. She had priced it ridiculously high to deter purchasers. It was special to her and she had wanted to keep it.

That painting, and the others in the collection, had saved her life. Creativity had brought healing. Art had healed her pain. But she was glad it was going to this quietly handsome, solid man with the commanding presence. There was something reassuringly familiar about him, something she couldn't quite place.

"Have we met before?" they both blurted.

Lucy shook her head, sending a curtain of blonde glossy hair sweeping across her backless little black dress. A smile fluttered to her lips, as in a reckless moment she wondered how soft his fingers would be, how supple they would feel, how sensuous the sound his skin upon her skin would be. Her body exploded in a heated flood of anticipation.

"I just, I don't know, there's something about you. Something familiar," he said.

His gaze locked with hers as though he'd sensed her

silent desire. Rather than look away she felt hypnotically drawn to his light.

"Yes, it's strange. I know, but I don't know," she said. There's something deliciously, reassuringly familiar, she thought.

"*Déjà vu,*" he said.

"What do you mean?"

"The feeling that one has lived the present situation before."

She felt suddenly adrift, like a ship in tumultuous seas.

"You're very knowledgeable about lighthouses," Lucy said, steering the conversation to solid ground, still intrigued by the depth of his earlier conviction.

"I should be. I was the lightkeeper at Pencarrow for three years," he hesitated and gazed at the painting.

Instinct told her something deeply personal had happened to him, something that could shed light on his own traumatic past.

"After my wife died," he offered by way of explanation, "My heart was ripped apart, and the only thing that saved me was running that lighthouse. It healed my heart."

A glaze of silent understanding united them muting the noise and clatter of the crowd, guiding them both away from the jagged coastlines of their shared sorrow, pain and hurt, to the deep still waters flooding their hearts.

"I am Anwar," he said, holding out his hand with a gesture that shouted royalty. "Anwar na Hassir," he added, looking at her as though searching for some sign of recognition that his name meant something to her.

Should it?

Anwar na Hassir? He was clearly from Arabic descent but beyond that she could not place him. She barely had time to troll through her memories before the gallery owner rushed to her side.

"Lucy, come and meet another buyer—if I may steal her away?" He added, aware of his intrusion.

She turned to leave. Their sacred union temporarily shattered by the ill-timed request.

"I'll take them all," Anwar said suddenly, with an air of explosive command.

"The paintings?" the gallery owner asked. "All of them?"

Lucy's pulse rate ricocheted as Anwar nodded his agreement. Had the paintings incited something deep within his soul, she wondered? Was that why he was buying out the whole exhibition? Was he a collector like many others in the gallery? A numbers man who prided himself on his many conquests and the number of artworks he possessed?

Lighthouses were rich with symbolism and conceptual meanings. She knew that better than anyone. Was the stranger attracted to the potent symbol of hope, rescue, refuge, safety and guidance? Was he offering her the same salvation, security, and strength? Or by buying her creations did he think she was also for purchase?

As the gallery owner scuttled away to tally his commission, Lucy gripped the edge of her catalogue, unsure whether to follow or stay.

No, she reassured herself, listening to her intuition as she studied him. Rising tall above her petite frame, he represented the best of man, he harbored the most lofty of ideals. His very proximity made her feel ever closer to the heavens and God. A towering signpost to guide the way which led to eternal love.

Anwar reached out, and gently caught her hand. He cupped his fingers around hers. Every whisper of hair on her body rose in heightened awareness.

"Don't go."

It was all she needed to hear. It was all she needed to know. It was all that she needed to believe.

Dreams do come true. And keepers are forever.

~

THE END

AFTERWORD

Have you ever experienced *déjà vu?* I think we all have at some time in our lives, whether it's a place, an event, or a person. There is much speculation as to how and why this phenomenon happens. But no-one has ever truly been able to explain it.

Some psychoanalysts attribute déjà vu to simple fantasy or wish fulfillment, while some psychiatrists ascribe it to a mismatching in the brain that causes us to mistake the present for the past. Then there's the intriguing view of parapsychologists who believe déjà vu is related to a past-life experience.

Obviously, there is more investigation to be done. But I have always believed that our dreams can come true, that our heart's hear and heal our tears, and that one day, regardless of our age and stage, our wounds and our fears, and the lovers that have crossed our paths, the right soul for our soul will appear...

And be a keeper.

THANK YOU

Thank you for reading *The Lightkeeper's Lover*... I hope you loved it. If you did...

1. Help other people find this book by writing a review
2. Signup for my new releases email to find out about the next book as soon as I release it, sign up here http://eepurl.com/ghM501
3. Email me at mollie@molliemathews.com with a copy of your honest review and let me know if you'd love to join my dream team and of advance readers
4. Follow me on BookBub, https://www.bookbub.com/authors/mollie-mathews
5. Stay in touch on Facebook, https://www.facebook.com/molliemathewsnz
6. Follow me on Twitter - https://twitter.com/Molliemathewsnz
7. Be inspired on Pinterest - https://nz.pinterest.

com/molliemathews and Instagram - https://
www.instagram.com/molliemathewsauthor

8. Follow my blog - https://molliemathews.
    wordpress.com

Keep reading for a preview of the first book in the Gemstone
Billionaire series, and sneak peeks into other passion-filled
stories including *Married By Christmas* and *Claimed by The
Sheikh*

ACKNOWLEDGMENTS

My sincere thanks to my beta readers for their enthusiastic cheerleading, and who read the preliminary chapters of this story and provided constructive feedback.

My special thanks to JoAnne and Pat, who have encouraged me to expand the ending to lead into a follow up to my Sheikh inspired stories—you'll find an excerpt from *Claimed By The Sheikh* in the pages that follow.

I loved the list of names for the hero in *The Lightkeeper's Lover*, that JoAnne sent me, inspired by her search of boys names that mean light. I went with Anwar. This Arabic name means 'light.

Thank you also to Andrew, a former U.S. Navy SEAL who inspired this story so many full-moons ago. Sadly, he never overcame the trauma of the things he experienced during his years of service, but he seems happy enough living on his own in an isolated part of New Zealand. The truth is, people can, and do, find happiness alone.

As Richard Bach, once wrote in *Jonathan Livingston Seagull,* "If you love someone, set them free. If they come back they're yours; if they don't they never were."

Andrew helped me learn that sometimes the love that is meant to last a lifetime is seldom the first person you meet, but a bridge across forever.

Would you enjoy listening to this story?

Did you enjoy reading this story? You may love the audiobook, written and narrated by me. Available now.

EXCERPT: MARRIED BY CHRISTMAS

MARRIED BY CHRISTMAS

What if the person who is so, so, so wrong for you is really so, so, so right, but you're too afraid to give love a chance?

Last Christmas art therapist Issy Riley was jilted by her fiancé. This Christmas she's running away. A week with a client on his private Fijian island promises to save her from cheating men and the London festive season. But when the client turns out to be a gorgeous and magnetic Italian billionaire, he threatens her resolve to never again trust her heart to the wrong man.

Milan fashion house leader and avowed bachelor Massimilliano Balforni has no intention of taking a vacation, despite his sister's insistence that he subject himself to an art therapy retreat following a minor heart attack. With an important collection due, he intends to fire his therapist and work, instead. But the determined and striking Issy gives his heart palpitations of a far more dangerous kind.

The one thing Max and Issy agree on: they are as wrong for each other as wrong gets. He's a workaholic playboy who believes emotion is a weakness. She's a romantic who yearns for a happily ever after.

As the tropical heat soars, they discover that in this battle between work and play, resistance only fuels attraction—and sometimes two wrongs make a very passionate right.

Set in two beautiful paradises—Milano, Italy and the tropical Pacific islands of Fiji.

(First published as The Italian Billionaire's Christmas Bride)

PRAISE FOR MARRIED BY CHRISTMAS

"A good read that takes you away to a tropical island to experience the steamy heat of two people determined to stay single in case they get hurt again. Max, a sexy, jaded Italian multi-billionaire meets up with Issy, a playful children's art therapist who has recently found out her fiancé was having an affair. Although I was initially skeptical as I usually go for historical romances, I'm glad I trusted my friend's recommendation because this book was delightfully compelling. The emotional vulnerabilities and character quirks combined with the sexual tension kept the pages turning. A frisky novel to curl up on the couch with or take away on your next trip."

~ Pauline Roberts

"This was a fun read I really enjoyed. It's perfect for a lazy weekend. This is the first book I have read by this author but it won't be last. I can't wait to be more."

~ Poppy

"Beautifully written. The author's vivid and descriptive writing style pulled me into a world I never wanted to leave. I loved the connection of art between two very different people and the healing it brought them both. A Very beautiful story!"

~ Hugh Harrison

"I joined Max to make the slow journey from betrayed broken-hearted individuals to the trusting and loving couple they become. Molly Mathew's writing transports you to places she is describing where you can kick back and relax for a while as this endearing story unfolds. Her characters soon become visible through her careful picture-building. Readers will like the Kiwi vernacular Issy invoices every now and then, and I think readers will enjoy getting to know the strong characters and the beautiful islands we're visiting. The author also tucks in some great life advice for everyone telling in the telling of this charming story. I hope you enjoy this book, too. I did."

~ Alfie Rues

"I loved, loved, loved this book. An instantly gripping, compelling and fun read. Escapism at its best. I couldn't put the book down and read it in one night. With exotic backdrops like Italy and Fiji and passionate characters, it made the perfect holiday read. Can kindness thaw a cold-heart? That's the question Mollie Mathews poses in her book about second chances and learning to love again.

Issy is a funny, compassionate art therapist who wants to escape Christmas after her jerk of a fiancé cheated on her.

Even though she only works with troubled children she agrees to take on a last minute client for her friend and business partner. What she doesn't know is her client is hunky fashion house CEO Massimilliano Balforni. Sparks fly and it's an attraction Max vows to deny. He doesn't want Issy and her colored pencils from bringing the wounds of his childhood to the light.

Mollie Mathews skillfully creates a gripping dynamic between Issy and Max that sensually blends their animosity with undeniable attraction making the tension soar. I definitely recommend this book."

~ Lauri

One word frees us
of all the weight
and pain of life:
That word is love
~ Sophocles

1

'*Che cavolo!* No! No! No! This will not do. Only an anorexic model could wear something that resembles a straw,' thundered Massimilliano Balforni, CEO of Emporio Balforni, Milan's most prestigious fashion house. His coal black brows knitted in a fierce line as he looked with disdain at the scatter of sketches the young designer splayed on Max's 15th Century walnut desk.

His protégé began to protest but one piercing look from the maestro forced his lips shut. His body stiffened as if frozen to the floor, reminded that his employer's wrath was more dangerous than black ice.

'Alexandria Gorbetz is a real woman, the world's richest woman, and someone like me that demands perfection.'

Max's mouth curved in a controlled smile. Was that fear he detected in the young man's face as Max pierced him with his dark gaze? He had every reason to be afraid. Enemies and friends alike knew Max had destroyed promising careers for lesser transgressions. Infinitesimal precision, extraordinary control, unrivaled beauty—Max suffered nothing less.

Pressing his fingertips to the smooth, cool parchment, he paused momentarily as a childhood memory stirred in his consciousness. He sucked in a breath and swept his hands brusquely across the page. He was no longer the lonely child who furtively sketched movie stars in beautiful clothes and dreamed of a Hollywood life.

What was once an escape was now a thriving commercial enterprise with insatiable demands. Max flourished his gold fountain pen across the page, adding a sweep of curves to the hips and breasts of the bespoke wedding gown his fashion house had been commissioned to design.

Now at the helm of his multi-billion dollar empire Max was no longer a hands-on designer, but nothing went out the door without his final veto. Some called him a control freak and this he took not as a criticism but as the highest compliment.

He waited to feel the rush of joy he used to feel when drawing as a child. He stopped to await the all-consuming love that arose from knowing that no one possessed his raw talent and genius. He paused to feel the pride that came years later from knowing he designed dresses perfectly, to satisfy only one client on her most important day. There was nothing.

It shouldn't have surprised him. He had long ago accepted that he was unable to feel the joy that other people did. He'd turned off that part of himself years ago and had vowed never again to succumb to vulnerability. In its place, carefully groomed aloofness and instilling fear in others were traits he prized and relentlessly cultivated.

As his protégé braced for the consequences Max forced his thoughts back to the commission. While he felt nothing in his heart, what he did experience as he looked at the drawing of the wedding dress executed to his design was a coolly detached appreciation that satisfied the perfectionist in him.

The lines and structure now conformed absolutely to his definition of ideal. The controlled steel gray pallet reflected his personality and every detailed aspect had been meticulously executed as he had commanded. No randomness or chaos anywhere.

Having witnessed his parents' brutal marriage and subsequent divorce, Max had no misguided notions of happily-ever-after, nor any desire to marry.

Perfection in relationships was simply unattainable. But the knowledge that he was at the helm of an empire that created exquisite, extraordinarily elegant gowns admired by the world's most elite, at the same time preserving a historic tradition, filled him with a degree of pride.

But as for the rest of his life—the personal, emotional side—he felt nothing. And that suited him perfectly.

Max's long supple fingers drummed an impatient rhythm on the armrest of his chair. '*Allora*?' Well? People react to fear, not love, he reminded himself as he kept his voice soft, but somehow containing all the might of the towering spires of the Duomo looming beyond his window.

A slither of fear crept into the young designer's hushed apology. 'I should have thought more about the woman beneath the dress.'

'Thinking is not enough,' Max commanded, his voice a dark, stark thing in the quiet of his office. 'You must apply.' Taking the drawings in both hands he tore the pages down the middle. 'Begin again, and this time bring me excellence.'

Ignoring the tiny pin like tremors piercing his chest Max pushed back from the desk and rose to his feet as the young man retrieved the torn fragments and scuttled quickly toward the door. Striding across the room Max willed his racing heart to cede to his control.

2

'Calm yourself, please Maxie,' Sophia Balforni said, sweeping into his office she cast the young man a sympathetic look as their paths crossed. 'Have you thought about what I suggested?' she asked, gesturing to the art therapy brochure peeking from beneath a pile of contracts.

'I am surrounded by amateurs and now you want me to play like a child, *mia sorella*. I have never heard something so ridiculous.'

'You're my brother. The best brother in the world, but do you know what's holding you back? You're afraid of losing control. You're afraid that without all of this, she said, sweeping her hand around the room, 'you're worthless.'

'But all of this means nothing if you're dead. And none of this means anything without someone to share your heart and soul. I hope one day you're able to realize that you're wonderful for who you are, not just for what you've accomplished. But most of all I hope you're able to experience the unconditional love and support of someone who loves you for you.'

Max was neither given to excessive emotion nor impetuousness but his mood wrestled with his need for control. He threw open the shuttered windows of his office and inhaled the frigid Milano air with shallow, measured breaths.

He ran his hand over his broad chest, fingering momentarily the fine scar snaking across his heart. His mind had the endurance and stamina of one thousand oxen but two months ago his body had betrayed him.

His gaze swept down the Piazza then flew up the spires of the Duomo, dusted with snow and bejeweled in dazzling pre-Christmas lights as the cacophony of Vespas buzzed like irritated wasps through the open window.

Although he had always hated Christmas, he loved tradition and he loved the supreme elegance that the Milanese never failed to deliver, but it pained him to concede that never had his beloved city been so irritating. In fact, everything, and everyone was irritating. Even his designs bored him. He knew better than most that he must continually innovate or die. Grudgingly he accepted his sister was right. He needed to get away.

'I admit it's a little unconventional,' Sophia said, taking an assortment of pills and vitamins from a gold embossed pillbox and, after pouring a glass of mineral water into a crystal tumbler, she passed the pills and water to Max.

'Unconventional?' Max tossed the pills into his mouth, took a gulp of water and threw back his head, grimacing as they slid down his throat. 'What you are suggesting is childish.' *Childish*, isn't that exactly what his father had thrown in his face when, as a young boy, he'd first shown him his sketches. 'If this got out to my competitors,' he said, forcing his mind from a memory he vowed never to revisit, 'can you imagine what it would do to my reputation?'

'Not nearly as damaging as being paralyzed by a stroke

and having to be spoon-fed, Sophia snapped. 'And since when have you cared what others think? Besides, you have an island on the other side of the world.

'One you've been too busy to visit. Fiji is remote enough for you to step away from the constant flash of cameras and be virtually anonymous,' she said, lowering her voice as Max's new PA cat-walked into his office. 'Call yourself Mr. Johnstone, or Mr. Smith, or whatever else you want, to protect your privacy.'

Beneath long-fringed lashes the PA gave Max a sultry look, trailing her gaze over his lean and muscled form, as she placed a collection of fashion magazines and media cuttings in a neat pile precisely as she'd been trained.

'Thank you, that will be all,' Sophia said, dismissing her.

'A nudist camp would be vastly more appealing,' Max's gaze trailed after his PA as she left his office. While he had no time for relationships, that didn't stop him from appreciating beauty. How much easier it would be to lie naked amongst a bevy of loveliness than expose his feelings to the spotlight.

Sophia rolled her eyes. 'I can just imagine what that would do to your blood pressure. Art, unlike making a career of intimately studying the curves of women, my dear brother, is therapeutic.'

'So you want me to go to kiddy school and make a fool of myself.' Irritation coursed through his veins as he ran his fingers around the neck of his shirt and loosened the starched white collar.

'You never had a childhood,' Sophia said, her voice almost a whisper. 'You grew up too fast. We both did. And now you're a thirty-five-year-old man who may not see forty.'

'I know you are trying to help but I told you I can handle

it.' And he would. He would never abandon his responsibility. Unlike his father who had tried to combine work with marriage and failed at both, Max had gladly sacrificed his personal life for his career.

Abandoned at birth by his biological parents, raised briefly by strangers, then dumped in a boarding school, he had turned what could have been a weakness into his biggest strength.

Self-reliance.

'All this stress has engulfed you, Max. Only you can't see it. And it scares me. You've become a shell of yourself—more than you were already. A man so cut off from his feelings that you are devoid of emotion. You've become a lighthouse of a man—lonely in a crowd, aloof and detached. Uncaring.'

The words bounced off Max's chest like the final shards of Milan's winter sun reflecting off the panoramic glass windows. It was true. He no longer cared.

'What do you want from me, Sophia?'

She paused, concern pooling in her dark eyes. 'I want what our mother wants. I want you to be happy.'

His lips curved in a tight mocking smile. When had his real mother ever cared about his happiness? He knew what she really wanted. After suddenly reappearing in his life, she wanted a daughter-in-law and she wanted a grandson. Max shook his head and gave a short exacerbated sigh. She wanted the impossible.

He plunged his hand through his hair, raking it back from his brow. He should have had it cut razor short last week. Instead, he'd thrown himself into the roll out of his retail network of 60 Massimilliano Balforni boutiques and jewelry stores throughout China, and the pending development of his luxury hotel in Dubai, with such single-minded, unrelenting focus there had been no time for indulgences.

'I've done my research,' he said, adding his signed consent to the final contracts, 'and from every angle it all seems based on spurious psychology.' His hand closed around the pen as he looked up sharply.

Sophia sucked her breath as though steeling herself to battle with his formidable will. 'Unless you make some changes, and I mean massive changes,' Sophia glanced momentarily in the direction of Cimitero Maggiore, Milan's largest cemetery, then fixed Max with a penetrating gaze, 'you'll end up like our father. *Morte.*'

'That will not happen to me,' he said, balling his fingers into a fist. 'I am nothing like our father.'

'No, you're not. You are loyal, honest and immensely generous to the people you care about—nothing like our father. But you are an unrelenting workaholic like he was. No better than an addict, because despite all your willpower, all your determination, all your talent, all your wealth you can't stop working. My God, you even live above your office.'

'*Mia sorella,* even if I wanted to go finger painting, which I do not, there is no way I can get away. People need me. I cannot just walk away without everything collapsing.'

'Even geniuses need time out to replenish. Super-heroes too,' she laughed. 'You, Clark Kent, need a rest from being Superman, a week out of this world. Not eternity. I will take care of things until you're back.'

The blood vessel in his temple pulsed, whether out of conviction or rebellion he didn't know, but her suggestion was not without merit. His sister had proven herself capable in so many ways since her appointment to Director of Public Relations.

He leaned back in his chair, steepling his fingers against

his lips as he savored a compelling idea. What if he could achieve several goals by leaving Italy? While he did not believe in fate, he did believe in destiny. Was it not destiny after all that had led him to this career, launching him from male model to CEO of a multi-billion dollar empire?

Max began to wonder if his recent conversation with some Fijian silk merchants was also pre-destined. Until that meeting he hadn't known there was such a large population of Indians in Fiji, and he'd been intrigued by the innovative textile developments they had shared with him.

And he could maximize efficiencies by going undercover and checking out his hotel chain in the Pacific. Yes, he thought, warming to the idea, perhaps a change of scene, getting away from all things European might just revive his flagging spirits.

His creativity was blocked, young designers were licking at his heels. He needed to continually innovate, but nothing inspired him. The plan was worth considering after all. Nothing else had worked. Plus it would get Sophia off his case. And the art therapy gimmick she was so convinced he needed?

What could any dowdy art therapist do to him that he couldn't control?

3

'First time to Fiji?' the porter asked art therapist Issy Riley as they wove past the rows of poolside loungers. Bronzed men and women wearing barely-there swimsuits tanned their lithe bodies beneath the last rays of the sun.

Issy was by far the most uniquely dressed, she thought euphemistically, gazing beyond the pool to the azure sea, fringed with coconut trees. Some, no doubt, would argue she was, in fact, the worst-dressed person at the resort, but then she'd never cared for fashion.

She pushed up the sleeves of the yellow shaggy pile of her jumper as two women sauntered past, tanned from crown chakra to pink toenails, their double d-cups jiggling like caramel panacottas.

Surrounded by an ocean of virtual nakedness Issy felt prudish dressed head-to-toenails in winter discomfort. Certainly less chic than the five-year old meandering past, resplendent in streaming caftan and matching overly bejew-eled sandals, snapping the sunset with her iPhone.

'Yes. First time anywhere overseas, actually,' she ran her fingers over the roll of her turtleneck, wishing she'd thought to wear a tee-shirt so she could peel the jumper off.

As always she'd left things too late. She'd been in a mad panic to get to the plane and hadn't even thought to pack spare clothes to change into once she'd arrived at Nadi airport.

Taking refuge beneath a palm tree Issy momentarily relaxed as a choir of Fijian men and women dressed in flowing white gowns began to sing in the open area just beyond the pool. Their voices soared through the humid air. Then suddenly realizing they were singing Christmas carols tension knotted her shoulders.

Christmas.

When she'd offered to help her business partner Nancy, and take this last minute client, she'd thought she could escape the festive season, dripping with tinsel and baubles, and the promise of happiness.

Her fingers tightened around the note the receptionist had passed her when she'd checked in. At least work meant she wouldn't have to spend the holiday season at her mother's with HIM—the traitorous, lying, three-timing control-freak of a fiancé. Make that ex-fiancé, she corrected. She had dumped him immediately, but that didn't stop her heart from taking a hit.

Issy stared into the distance her attention diverted by a huge Christmas tree blazing with a rainbow of colored lights. She closed her eyes and sighed. Why couldn't she find a promise-keeper?

Married by Christmas? Nope. Once again the bus of happily-ever-after failed to pull up at her stop, but to find out on Facebook that James was cheating on her weeks before their wedding? No one deserved that humiliation.

Even if her mother still thought James was the best thing since sliced toast, at least Issy had the balls to shut down his lies, the courage to confront the truth, the strength to face life on her own again. She swallowed hard as the sharp edge of betrayal ran a ragged line through her chest. She'd had a lucky escape.

The porter smiled stiffly as though sensing her discomfort. 'Holiday?'

Issy looked longingly at people relaxing by the pool, her gaze hovering over a loved-up couple entwined on a sun-lounger. She felt a tug of disappointment. Would she ever trust enough to fall in love again? She crushed the note from her client in her hands, pressing her lips together as she turned away. 'Business.'

All the men in her life, even her father, had let her down terribly. Work was a most welcome distraction. She didn't need a man in her life, she reminded herself. Not anymore.

A riot of shouts from the beach pulled her attention toward a group of men jabbing at something writhing on the sand at the edge of the lagoon. Whether it was an instinctive sense of brutality etched in the men's postures or the impact of the powerful figure brushing past her, she didn't know, but every whisper of her body hair stood erect.

Issy watched mesmerized, adrenaline lapping her body as a 6 foot 3 Adonis with olive toned six-pack abs and a body that could easily grace a billboard strode toward the men on the beach, clad only in tiny trunks.

He looked strangely familiar in an unfamiliar sort of way, like a celebrity in a magazine, the same handsomeness, and aloof assurance, although she knew she'd never met him before. He looked like a movie star, only tougher? Certainly not a man anyone would forget.

His muscles rippled gold fire under the heat of the

fading tropical sun as, with powerful, lithe steps like a panther about to lunge, the titan advanced upon the men on the beach. Fear shadowed their faces as they turned to each other, eyes widening, aware this was no normal man approaching but a warrior, a leader of men, a man not to be defied.

'*Allora*! Stop!' His rich honey-toned voice, edged with a deep sultry Italian accent, sent shivers coursing through her body.

Tearing her eyes away from this perfect specimen of a man Issy perched on her toes, squinting under the bright sun to see what the titan was so vigorously trying to protect.

'Sea snake. Very poisonous,' the porter said.

Danger.

The warning flashed red in her mind and jackknifed through the air. Was it the snake she was afraid of or the rush of molten emotion the stranger incited?

'Come and see,' the porter beckoned.

She hesitated, torn between fear and fascination. Her pulse hammered, pummeled by the unexpected handsomeness of the man and stricken with curiosity. What sort of person would go to a snake's rescue?

For the first time in forever she felt excited, alive, her body on edge, ablaze. Why, when she was officially off men, and as she walked toward him did every whisper of hair on her body stand alert?

She frowned, trying to remember any man ever having inflamed such a reaction, as his muscular arms took the sticks from the assailants. Arms that could crush an opponent or protect a woman against his powerful lean body.

'We're only trying to protect the resort guests from danger,' the men shouted.

'*Che cavolo*! Can you not see the baby snake?' he jabbed

his finger towards the rocks. 'Would you deprive it of its mother?' His eyes were a lethal shade of gunpowder blue, his gaze unyielding, freezing the men in a chilly silence. 'She will not strike unless provoked.'

Issy's breath caught in ragged gasps as she glanced at the tiny snake lingering in the distant shadows. Was this guy for real? Someone like her, who cared nothing for the senseless killing of animals.

'We didn't see it. We didn't think,' they said, stepping back. 'Sorry, Sir.'

Issy smiled, her body flooding with something that felt uncomfortably like admiration. She dragged her eyes from him and focused on the snake lying washed ashore, exposed in its vulnerability.

As dangerous as the snake was alleged to be the artist in her was captivated by the beauty of its iridescent pearl and obsidian stripes. But she was wary too, of its potent power. Was the snake feigning death or was it spellbound, against its will, offering herself to the giant of a man before her?

Issy's heart seemed to freeze then pounded like the sea crashing on the distant reef. She could relate to feeling out of her depth. She stole a glance at the knight without armor standing in far too skimpy trunks as with soft, deft movements that belied his powerful physique, he gently nudged the snake toward the sea.

Issy kept her gaze firmly on the snake as it uncoiled slowly, writhing in the wet sand as Issy drew closer to its rescuer. She stood a body's length away from him, agonizingly aware of the rich luster of his full head of blue-black wavy hair, his impeccably shaven jaw, and the intoxicating aroma of his cologne coiling through the balmy air. Earthy, sensual, exhilarating.

What was up with that, she wondered bamboozled by

the commotion clanging through her mind. Her eyes recklessly savored every contoured edge of the Adonis's body as he stood at the water's edge watching the snake slither to freedom. She traced his broad, bronzed, well-oiled chest, before sliding down the tantalizingly playful coils of soft dark hair dividing his sculptured six pack and marching a confident line from his navel, before vanishing below the rim of his tiny 'spray on' trunks.

Suddenly the Adonis turned toward her and she was immediately captured in the web of his intense blue eyes.

Issy looked away quickly. Too quickly.

Sprung!

Her face flamed carmine red as she studied her feet, wishing the escaping waves of rose pink hair that fell over her face as she did so would hide her indefinitely. After a brief moment she glanced up, hoping he had not read her mind when she'd gawked at him. The smirk on his face and the intensity of his gaze left her in no doubt he'd registered her attraction.

'Thank you for saving the snake Mr Johnstone,' said the porter, offering him a towel as he went to his side.

'Johnstone?' her voice eked out. Her eyes ping-ponged between the stranger and the porter. Thrusting her hand in her pocket, she unfurled the note the receptionist had given her. Issy's stomach dived a nervous somersault that would have done an Olympic swimmer proud as she reread the message, studying the words forged in firm, confident handwriting—no sign of weakness anywhere. "Meet me by the pool. (Signed) Mr. Johnstone."

Oh, God. Mortification coiled through her body. 'You can't be *that* Mr. Johnstone.'

He stared at her as if she was insane.

She bit her lip, holding back any attempt at an explanation for her earlier behavior that she knew would only dig a deeper hole. 'There must be some mistake.'

DID YOU ENJOY READING THIS EXCERPT

Did you enjoy reading this excerpt?
Married by Christmas is available now in eBook and Print
from all good online bookstores.

Read on for a sneak peek into Mollie's upcoming book
Claimed by The Sheikh

Claimed
By The Sheikh
MOLLIE
MATHEWS

CLAIMED BY THE SHEIKH

BOOK TWO IN THE TRUE LOVE SERIES.

Available now

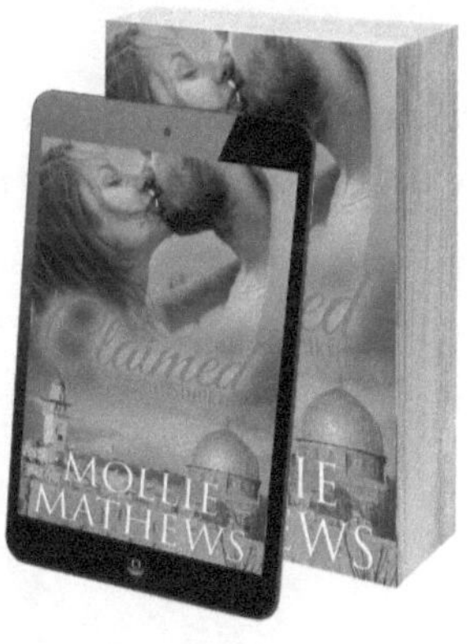

A grief-stricken Sheikh Tariq na Hassir, the formidable ruler of the Kingdom of Avana, arrives in Paris to claim his brother's child after a car crash killed his parents--only to find out from the hospital that the child isn't their biological son. It's Tariq's son, with his former lover.

Three years ago, after being banished by Tariq from his desert kingdom, renown architect Melanie Jones secretly gave her baby to Tariq's childless brother and his wife, in a swap the world was never supposed to discover.

The tragedy pulls her back to the world that rejected her and the man who abandoned her—the only man capable of tuning her carefully controlled world upside down.

Tariq will do whatever it takes to protect his legacy, including claiming Melanie as his bride and his son as heir before scandals ensue. But Melanie has other plans for her future—a westernized life where she's free to operate her own business and control her own life.

Join Mollie's new release newsletter here http://eepurl.-com/cigEsH. Be the first to know when *the next book in the series* is released.

1
____

"Are you trying to kill her?" Tariq na Hassir, the formidable ruler of the Kingdom of Avana, seized the animal handler's arm, forcing him to release the rope laced around the baby giraffe's neck.

"She has suffered enough trauma." Tariq dismissed the man with a fierce scowl that stuck fear into enemies.

A slither of panic crept into the young man's hushed apology. "I am sorry your Excellency."

"Release the others from their cages," Tariq growled.

The man did not have to be asked twice. He knew from experience that the Sheikh's retribution for disobedience would be swift and merciless.

"You are safe from harm," Tariq said softly, stroking the baby giraffe's long neck with a gentleness that belied his strength.

"No one will ever hurt you again, Noor," he said softly, impulsively naming her as his fingertips swept through the calf 's fur. He let his long supple fingers linger a moment upon her tail. Thankfully they had saved her in time, he thought as he reached for the reins, clenching his powerful hands around the soft leather.

The rage he had first felt on hearing about the ruthless murder of the new born's mother still roared through him. Had she been executed to pay a tail dowry to the father of some money-mongering bride, he wondered? Or did some heinous person pay thousands of dollars for a wretched fly swatter?

Noor looked up and met Tariq's dark gaze. In her innocent eyes, he saw her despair, her disillusionment, her disgust with humanity. He recognized her trauma as though it was his own. Because it was.

"Humans," he said, his voice marinated with contempt. "The people you should be able to trust, the people who say they care, the people whose actions should be driven by love —the majority are driven by nothing but selfishness, deception, and lies."

Taking a bottle of milk, he placed the teat to Noor's lips. The calf's silky black lashes grazed her cheeks as she gazed down at the foreign object then looked back at Tariq. She stared silently up at him, her eyes moist and bewildered.

Tariq had trained himself to shut down his emotions but that skill suddenly failed him. His chest trembled with suppressed rage knowing the orphaned baby would never again taste her mother's milk.

"What passes for love among some people is abhorrent," he said in a low, strained voice. "On behalf of humanity, I apologize."

The killing of the calf's mother and three other rare Kordofan giraffes by trophy hunters seeking their tails further motivated the Sheikh's commitment to transform his anger into action.

"Do you really think you can save her?"

Tariq looked at Anwar, his younger brother by 11 months. His head was slightly bowed but he could see his eyes were fixed in sadness and longing.

Tension ripped down Tariq's spine. "Our father's reign of terror and tyranny have robbed Avana of prosperity and peace. I will make it my personal mission to right the injustices of the past. War and hostility must end. And it starts with how we treat those most vulnerable."

His fingers shook as he gripped the bottle of milk as Noor, at last, began to suckle.

An eerie silence swept across the precipitous landscape of Avana's Tiwa oasis. Tariq lifted his gaze to the horizon. The only movement visible to his naked eye was the wind etching a delicate furrow as it crawled over the golden dunes.

"Not only will I provide a sanctuary for hunted wildlife and orphans like Noor, but I will liberate God's most precious creatures from the many closing zoos and other inhumane habitats around the world," he glanced over at the other animals being unloaded from the custom-built crates.

"I will create a world-acclaimed sanctuary, impenetrable by those with impure and malicious hearts. It will be the most magical, marvelous, mesmerizingly unique place, the number one eco-tourism destination in the world. I will create meaningful employment for our people, restoring their dignity, attracting millions of visitors annually and contributing billions to the economy. But more importantly, I will show the world how kindness and compassion can be turned into plutonium and change the world."

Anwar glanced at the now lush landscape and recalled

how barren it had once been. With no sign of life in sight, others had found it impossible to fathom his brother's vision to transform the punishing and unforgiving conditions into a haven for so many endangered species. Yet, as with everything Tariq turned his formidable will and mind-blowing wealth to, he had succeeded where mere mortals were destined to fail.

Anwar's heart swelled with pride as he thought of all his brother's achievements. "It's an audacious and admirable plan. And if anyone can pull it off it's you, brother. Your passion, your drive, your unrelenting ambition and pursuit of goals exceeds mere mortals. And you have the endurance and power of 13,000 Arabian horses, but aren't you setting yourself up for too much hard work? Why don't you relax? Kick back. Enjoy the fruits of your reign?" Anwar said, tossing his head in the direction of the harem. "Other men would."

"Women were our father's weakness," bitterness bled from his words. "I too once made the same mistake. I too paid the price."

There was a tense silence while Tariq lifted his gaze to the sky and studied the giant falcon circling above.

"Was it not you who once taught that your greatest weakness can also be your greatest strength?" Anwar asked.

Tariq shook his head, biting down a terse retort. "I was misled." He said, nodding his command to the animal handler lingering at a respectful distance.

He petted Noor as she was led away. "All kinds of atrocities are committed in the name of love, which is why it is the most dangerous of emotions, and why I am forever turned off to women."

* * *

Claimed by the Sheikh, book two in the True Love series series available now from all good bookstores.

ABOUT THE AUTHOR

MOLLIE MATHEWS writes fun, sophisticated, passion-filled contemporary romance. She is known for her "sensual, beautiful, empowered stories enveloped in true romance" (5-star review). Her books have resonated with a global audience. She has been featured in magazines, television, and radio.

A former child and family therapist Mollie passionately believes in the power of romance to transform people's lives. She loves Mother Theresa's words, *"We are all pens in the hands of a writing God sending love letters to the world."*

Her stories are unashamedly positive, optimistic, full of fun and passion.

She is graduate of Victoria University, in Wellington, New Zealand and has given keynote speeches at romance writers conventions and international seminars.

Mollie follows the sun, dividing her time between New Zealand and exotic locations—wherever she intends setting her next romance novel. She lives with her very own romantic hero, Lorenzo—tall, dark, terribly handsome and fluent in Spanish!

Follow her on BookBub https://www.bookbub.com/authors/mollie-mathews and on her blog https://molliemathews.wordpress.com

and sign up for Mollie's newsletter at www.Molliemathews.com and receive her FREE gift.

BY MOLLIE MATHEWS

GEMSTONE BILLIONAIRE BRIDES:

*THE ITALIAN BILLIONAIRE'S CHRISTMAS
    BRIDE*

*THE ITALIAN BILLIONAIRE'S SCANDALOUS
    MARRIAGE*

*GEMSTONE BILLIONAIRES 2 BOOK-
    BUNDLE BOX SET*

*GEMSTONE BILLIONAIRES 3 BOOK-
    BUNDLE BOX SET*

PASSION DOWN UNDER:

MARRIED BY CHRISTMAS
BRIDE OF GOLD

TRUE LOVE:

FLIGHT of PASSION
CLAIMED by THE SHEIKH

PASSION DOWN UNDER SASSY SHORT
     STORIES:

TWIST OF FATE
LOVE ME FOREVER
LOVE ME AS I AM
FOREVER AND ALWAYS
THE LIGHTKEEPER'S LOVER
PASSION DOWN UNDER 2 BOOK-BUNDLE
     BOX SET (Books 1 & 2)
PASSION DOWN UNDER 3 BOOK-BUNDLE
     BOX SET (Books 1, 2 & 3)

New Zealand

Visit www.molliemathews.com to read more about all our books and to buy them. You will also find features, author interviews and news of author events, and you can sign up for e-newsletters so that you're always first to hear about our new releases.

❀ Created with Vellum